Tales of a Pirate Ninja

Daniel Kenney

Chapter One

My name is Archie Beller, and this is my tale. Okay, that sounds weird. It sounds like I have something growing out of my rump. I told Eduardo that I should call it my 'story' instead of my 'tale.' He insisted that 'tale' was more refined and sophisticated than 'story.' I have no idea why he thinks I need this to sound refined and sophisticated because, you know, the truth is—I'm just a ninja. A pirate ninja.

Nothing very refined and sophisticated about that.

Confused?

Don't be. I'll start at the very beginning so you know every detail of this cosmic tale. And when I say that, I don't mean I have a star-sized tail growing out of my you-know-what; I mean I have many stories to tell, and this is just the first.

School had already been in session for two weeks when I arrived at the steps of Kingman School in Kings Cove, California. Why two weeks late, you ask? Long story about my mom and her job that I'd rather not get into. Let's just say it was complicated.

This was my third new school since Kindergarten, because

my mom's life often got 'complicated.' But that's okay, whatever made her happy. Plus, I was always pretty good at making friends.

At least, that was what I thought as I stood at the bottom of Kingman's steps. When my mom dropped me off, it was as if the entire student body stopped what they were doing. They stared at me like I was some freakish zoo animal.

Welcome to California.

I found my way to the office and met Principal Adelhart, who then walked me down the hallways and introduced me to my new teacher, Mrs. Munderson. Munderson was tall and pretty – for a teacher, that is. She motioned for me to stand at the front of class and then invited me to say hello to everyone for one humiliating moment. The kids in class all exchanged funny glances, like I might be from outer space, and I was hopeful the worst was over. I sat down at the only empty desk, right smack dab in the middle of the room. As I grabbed a notebook and pen, I scanned the room and assessed my situation. At first glance, it appeared California kids looked a lot like Nebraska kids. There was nothing to worry about. This would go just fine.

At 11:30, the bell rang and the students lined up to go to lunch. Mrs. Munderson smiled and told me not to worry, just follow everybody else.

No problem.

I followed the horde to the cafeteria, grabbed my lunch and milk, scanned the room, and saw a group of guys that looked somewhere between normal and cool. A group I could hang with. I walked over.

"You guys mind if I sit with you?"

The boy at the end looked down at the others. A couple kids shrugged back, then he looked back at me. "Sure," he said.

I sat down and they all returned to their own food and conversations. Not exactly the warmest welcome, but they'd come around. I poked at my salad a bit and then dove into my mac and cheese when the skinny boy with big ears across from me started to talk.

"So, uh, what was your name again?" he asked.

"Archie," I said. "Archie Beller."

"So, where are you from, Archie?" he asked.

"Omaha," I said.

I heard chairs move in that uncomfortable way. Several kids exchanged strange looks.

"What's Omaha?" one of them asked.

I laughed, then stopped when I noticed none of them were laughing.

"Is it a country?" one of them asked another.

"No, idiot," said one of the kids in the middle. He had floppy black hair and wore a sneer on his face. He looked my way. "It's a state, right?"

I started to laugh but then caught myself. These guys were serious.

"Um, no," I said. "Omaha is a city inside the state of Nebraska."

They all looked at me blankly.

"And Nebraska is a state that lies within the United States of America."

"For real?" one of them asked.

"Huh," said one guy as he made a sour face. "Who knew?"

Pretty much every American who can read a map, is what I wanted to say. But I didn't. These California kids may just be a little bit different after all. I went back to eating my mac and cheese and the other kids went back to their conversations. I needed a different approach.

I coughed until skinny with big ears looked at me. "So, ummm…"

"Mike. My name's Mike," he said.

"So, Mike, who's your favorite super hero?" I said.

"Favorite superhero?" he asked with a confused look.

"Yeah, are you more of a Batman, Spiderman, or Superman guy? I mean, I won't hate you if you like Superman but I won't have much respect for you either, if you know what I mean." I chuckled and he gave me the world's most clueless face.

"What are you talking about?" he said.

I shrugged. "You know. Superheroes? In comic books and in movies? Did you like Avengers? Are you psyched for the next Iron Man?"

"Dude," he finally said. "I'm not into superheroes. I like ninjas."

"Ninjas?" I said.

The chairs did that uncomfortable thing again as the entire table turned my way.

"Did someone say ninjas?" the floppy haired boy in the middle asked. "I thought we agreed about this."

Mike pointed at me. "It was the new kid, McGinley, I swear it."

Floppy haired McGinley looked at me. "Is that true?" he said.

I was so confused. "Yeah, I said the word ninjas but only after Mike said the word. I asked him who was his favorite superhero and he said he liked ninjas."

"We're not into superheroes around here," McGinley said.

"So you don't read comic books?" I asked.

"Arrr," the kid across from him said. "We're into pirates around here.'"

McGinley shot out of his seat. "No, we're not," he hissed. "We're into ninjas around here."

Now both sides of the table stood up. Half of the kids shouted pirates and the other half shouted ninjas.

I felt like I'd entered an alternative universe. But then I remembered. It was only California.

After the end of lunch bell rang, kids scattered from their tables, dumped their empty trays through a hole in the wall, and hustled outside.

I trailed the others, thinking about how things had gone. I had to admit, I'd had better first days in the lunchroom. I took a deep breath of the warm California air. At least it was recess time. I just needed to find a game, stay on the edges, and at least for the rest of the day, try not to do anything else that these California kids might think was weird.

The boys from my grade had assembled into two groups at one end of the parking lot. I wondered if they might be getting ready to play football so I walked towards them, ready to play.

That floppy haired McGinley kid stepped out from the bunch on the left. The kid who said "Arrr," stepped out from the bunch on the right.

"So, Archie from Omaha," said McGinley, "what side is it going to be?"

"Yeah," said the other kid. "Which side?"

I clapped my hands and rubbed them together. "You guys tell me: we playing football or soccer?"

McGinley and the other kid exchanged a weird look, then they turned back towards me.

"Don't play dumb with us," said McGinley. "It's very simple. Are you going to hang with us ninjas or are you going to hang with those loser pirates?"

"Arrrr," the other kid said again. "Them's fighting words, McGinley. Fighting words, I say."

"Shut it, Barry," said McGinley.

I was confused.

"Guys, I don't have any idea what you're talking about."

"Well, I guess that means you Omaha kids are pretty slow. It's simple." He jabbed his thumb into this chest. "We're into ninjas and, because they're insane, they are into pirates. So, Archie, you gotta choose: ninjas or pirates?"

"What do you mean, I gotta choose?"

"Arrr," said Barry. "Unless you want to be hanging out with the Nimrods over in Loserville, you gotta make a choice." He pointed behind me.

I spun and looked. In the distance, hanging around a light pole, were four kids. They had to be the four goofiest kids I'd ever seen in my life. Nimrods. I spun back around.

"But I don't know anything about ninjas or pirates. I'm into comic books and superheroes. Heck, I even like football players and basketball players. I have some trading cards … I could bring 'em tomorrow."

That apparently was funny because both groups of boys started laughing. Then finally, McGinley and Barry looked at me.

"Arr, wait, you're serious?" said Barry.

"Listen, Archie," said McGinley. "I don't know what life was like back in Omaha, but around here, we're into ninjas."

"Pirates," hissed Barry.

"And here's the deal," said McGinley. "Wednesday night,

there's a fall bonfire to kick off the new school year. All the kids in school will be there. It's a costume sort of a thing. You make your decision by then. If you're with us, you'll come dressed like a ninja."

"Arrrr," Barry said. "And if you've got an ounce of sense in that pea brain of yours, you'll come dressed like a pirate."

McGinley and Barry turned from me, held each other's gaze for a long moment, then spun around. The two groups walked away from each other. I stared in bewilderment as the ninja group started practicing what looked like karate moves and the pirates started yelling ahoy in unison.

There was no doubt about it. I had definitely entered an alternate universe. Then I remembered. It was only California.

Chapter Two

Over the next two days, I kept to myself at school. I tried to catch up in my classes, ate alone during lunch, and sat on the curb watching everybody else at recess. It was so weird how pirates stuck with pirates, how ninjas stayed with ninjas, and how four booger eaters known as the Nimrods hung around a light pole.

And I had a choice to make.

Back in Omaha, I went to a normal school, where I was just a normal kid with normal friends. We would talk about our favorite movies, exchange comic books, play football, play video games. That kind of stuff.

But these California kids?

Let's just say they took this ninja vs. pirate stuff way too seriously. And after school, McGinley and Barry stopped me in the hall.

"Remember, Archie from Omaha," McGinley said. "Bonfire. Tonight. You make your decision or you spend the rest of your life with the Nimrods."

"Arrrr," said Barry. "'Tis that clear enough for ya?"

"Crystal," I said.

But, of course, I was the farthest thing from crystal clear on the matter. I took some money that I'd saved up and rode my bike to a costume store after school. I looked at all the ninja costumes. I looked at all the pirate costumes.

I couldn't make up my mind.

So I bought both.

I decided to go home, try on both outfits, figure out what I liked best, and make my decision that way.

But by the time I got home, Mom was already there. She'd come home from work early and had Chinese takeout on the table.

She smiled one of her big cheesy smiles and clapped her hands together. "Thought we'd celebrate our first week. Whaddya say, Archie? You me, Chinese, and a movie?"

"Yeah, well, that sounds great, Mom, but there's a school bonfire tonight and I kinda gotta go."

Her eyes got big and she clenched her fists. Then she started shaking her head as she opened her arms up wide.

Mom was coming in for a hug.

"Oh, my Archie's making friends already. School-wide bonfire?" She grabbed me and squeezed, and rocked me back and forth. "Oh, Archie, I knew coming to California would be good for us. Yes, go to your bonfire. We can do movie night tomorrow, okay?"

I went to my room, and locked the door. It was time to make a decision. I slipped on my ninja outfit first and checked myself out in the mirror. Not bad, I thought. I would have preferred a Batman costume, but not bad at all.

Time for the pirate costume. I put all of it on, then finished with the eye patch and pirate hat. Once again, I checked myself out. I guess I was hoping that when I put on both costumes, I would somehow know the right decision. As if one would fit better or be cooler than the other. But the truth? It kinda felt like a tie.

And I knew, a tie wouldn't work for the weirdoes of Kingman School. I needed to choose a side, or face permanent banishment to the light pole of the Nimrods.

I slipped the ninja outfit back on, then the pirate, then the ninja, then the pirate. It was more of a tie than ever before and I was so confused.

Finally, I put the ninja outfit back on and then started to put the pirate outfit on over it.

I looked at myself again and laughed.

A Pirate Ninja.

Honestly, that was way cooler than these ninjas and pirates.

"Honey," my mom called from the living room. "You're gonna be late for your bonfire. Are you sure you don't need a ride?"

What did she think I was, a fourth grader? I was in fifth grade, I owned my own bike, and I could handle myself on the streets, even if it was California.

I took another look in the mirror. Decision time.

But after staring at myself for what seemed like an eternity…I just couldn't do it. I wasn't yet prepared to make quite possibly the biggest decision of my young life, whether to spend the rest of my middle school days as a ninja or a pirate.

I took a deep breath.

"Honey, you're going to be late!" my mom said again from the living room.

Then I had a really stupid idea. And in my experience, most of my greatest ideas were stupid. I needed to get out. My clearest thinking – usually my best thinking – got done while riding my bike. If I was going to commit one way or the other, I needed to make my decision on the move. Then, I would change into the proper costume before getting to the bonfire.

Yep, definitely the dumbest idea I'd ever had.

I hollered to my mom that I was leaving, then snuck out the back so she couldn't see me in my ridiculous costume. I jumped on my bike and was off.

The evening air was cool, surprisingly cool. I always thought of California as hot, but truth was, Nebraska was way hotter. And, from what I knew about California, Nebraska was way colder. Kings Cove, California was just about right. Temperature wise, that is. The people were weird.

Unfortunately, the bike ride and the cool air didn't get me any closer to a decision. And so there I was pedaling down the street towards Kingman. Even from a distance, I could spot a very bright bonfire up ahead.

And then I heard someone scream.

It was a girl. She screamed again. Scratch that – a woman.

I squinted and, through my ninja mask, saw a woman falling down on the concrete as some big dude pulled at her purse.

I know I should have stopped pedaling and called the police, but for some reason, I didn't.

Maybe it was all those years of reading comic books and going to super hero movies, but something inside me wasn't scared.

I wanted to help this woman.

And that's when I saw who it was.

Mrs. Munderson. My teacher!

The guy was dragging that purse and Mrs. Munderson

wouldn't let go so now the guy was dragging her.

And nobody else but me was seeing this.

I had to do something.

I had to do something now!

I slammed my foot down on my pedal and pedaled like crazy towards Munderson and the thief. I rode as fast as my legs could take me. I was pretty good at riding bikes and could do it no-handed, no problem. So that was what I did. I took my hands off the handlebars, grabbed my fake ninja sword out of its sheath, and readied it above my shoulders. Then as I got close, I screamed the only thing that popped into my head, "Ahoy Matey!" and I leaped from my bike right at that dirtbag. He looked up as I came flying through the air, and I let loose with my fake ninja sword, and hit him across the forehead.

He fell backwards and onto his back. I landed on the ground, rolled over, popped up to my feet, and lifted the fake sword above my head. "Time for you to walk the plank!" I yelled even though that didn't make any sense at all. The adrenaline had taken over, what could I say?

The guy screamed and covered his face. He clearly thought I had a real sword. Then he started crawling backwards and scrambled to his feet. He sprinted away. But about twenty feet away, he turned around and wagged his finger at me.

"When I find out who you are, I'll get you!" he yelled.

Get me? I swallowed hard. And the moment I thought about going after him passed without my moving. Then I remembered. There was a victim. Mrs. Munderson! I let the scary dude get away, and turned back towards Munderson. She was clutching her purse and looking up at me.

"Thank you," she said to me with tears in her eyes.

I didn't know what to say and all that came out was, "Arrrr."

I held my hand out and she took it. I helped her to her feet.

"You saved me," she said. "You're a hero." She reached out to me but I backed away. "Who are you?" she asked.

I wanted to say something. I wanted to answer her, but I couldn't. I didn't know what to say. I froze. Then I panicked. I grabbed my bike, jumped on, and instead of riding to the bonfire, I rode the other direction.

Mrs. Munderson jogged after me but I was way too fast. "Who are you?" she yelled.

Who was I?

Just a boy from Omaha, riding his bike, wearing a Pirate Ninja costume. That's who.

Chapter Three

I stopped by an all-night diner called Super Donut, grabbed a hot glazed, and sat down and read the comic book I'd stuffed in my back pocket. The college guy making donuts looked at me all weird, but I didn't care. Heck, if ninjas and pirates were such a big deal to the people of Kings Cove, how weird could a Pirate Ninja really be? After an hour, I headed home. I slipped in the back and Mom hollered at me from her room, asking how it went.

"Great," I said.

She squealed in delight, and I hurried to my room, buried my head in my pillow, and fell asleep.

As soon as I entered school the next morning, I knew something weird was going on. The kids were excited, talking like something had happened. Several were holding newspapers. I went to my locker, grabbed my books, and headed to first period.

I saw Mrs. Munderson as soon as I entered class. She was at her desk and noticed me at once. She nodded but nothing else. No recognition.

Whew. I was in the clear.

After the Pledge of Allegiance, Mrs. Munderson started to talk. A dozen or so hands immediately shot into the air, which was strange since she hadn't yet asked any questions. She rolled her eyes and called on a boy in the front.

"Yes Jimmy, what is it?"

"Is it true Mrs. Munderson, what the paper said?"

She sighed and her shoulders fell forward. "Yes, Jimmy, it's true."

"Can you tell us what happened?" asked Veronica from the back.

"Well," Mrs. Munderson said with her hands now stuck into her hips, "if you read the paper, then you already know what happened."

Another girl's hand shot up. I think it was Cindy. "Please, Mrs. Munderson? Please?"

Mrs. Munderson rolled her eyes. "Fine. If you all must know, I was on my way to the bonfire when some thug knocked me down and tried to steal my purse. Anyways, some brave person came riding along on their bike and fought off my attacker. I was okay, I kept my purse, and the thug ran away. There's really nothing else to say."

McGinley jabbed a finger into the paper he'd spread out on his desk. "But you told the police that—"

Mrs. Munderson cut him off with her hand. "Yes, I told the police that the brave person who fought off the attacker was dressed in a costume."

"What kind of costume?" asked McGinley.

Munderson looked around, then ran her tongue along her

17

top lip. She sighed one more time. "A Pirate Ninja costume."

"A Pirate Ninja!" the whole class shouted at once.

"Which was it Mrs. Munderson?" asked McGinley. "You can either be a ninja, because you're cool, or a pirate because you're a dork, but not both. Which was it?"

"First, Mr. McGinley, you are not to use the word dork in my class. Secondly, I know what I saw. The person who saved me was both a pirate and a ninja. A Pirate Ninja. He bravely fought off my attacker, and then rode away. I barely had a chance to thank him."

"How do you know it's a *him*?" asked Sally. "Maybe Pirate Ninjas are all girls."

"A good point, Sally. Fact is, I don't know who it was. All I know is that a brave Pirate Ninja saved me *and* my purse last night. And I'm greatly indebted. Now class, if that's all, we can begin."

But that wasn't all. In fact, for the next two and a half hours, the Pirate Ninja of Kings Cove, California was all anybody could focus on. And then finally, the lunch bell rang.

I followed the others out of class and down to the cafeteria. I grabbed my tray. I had to admit, this Pirate Ninja deal was way bigger than I'd ever expected. Part of me wanted to stand up and admit it was me. Maybe that would make them all like me. But I'd also read enough comic books to know that the moment people know the identity of the super hero, bad things would happen.

In fact, that thug told me he'd get me.

Nope, it was better to keep quiet.

I grabbed an extremely soggy slice of pizza and scanned the cafeteria for someplace to sit.

McGinley and Barry rolled up on me.

"So, Archie from Omaha," said McGinley, "we didn't see you at the bonfire last night."

"Arrrr," said Barry, "we pirates didn't see you, neither. Figured you'd joined them scurvy ninjas."

"One last chance, Archie, right here, right now. Who you gonna choose: ninja or pirate?"

This was completely ridiculous. "Guys, I don't understand why I have to choose. Why can't I be friends with both of you?" I said.

McGinley shook his head at me. "I knew it," he said, his voice dripping with contempt.

Barry nodded. "Arrr, Mac, for once I agree with you. Archie here's definitely a booger eater."

McGinley laughed. "Have fun with the Nimrods." He started walking away when suddenly he stopped and turned around real slow.

"Wait a second," he said. "Wait just a second." He jabbed his finger at me. "You weren't at the bonfire last night and *now* you can't decide between being a pirate and a ninja." He looked at Barry.

"Arrr, I see where you going with this, Mac. So what of it newbie? Are you maybe the Pirate Ninja?"

Things in the cafeteria suddenly seemed very quiet. I swallowed hard.

"Me?" I said. "Ha, ha, ha. Guys, that's funny."

Mac tilted his head. "Is it?"

"Yeah, two things. For one, take a good look at me. Do I look like the kind of kid that's a hero?"

They both studied me.

"Seriously, guys?" I said.

Barry's face finally relaxed into a smile. "Arrr, Mac, me thinks this land-lover has a good point."

Mac rolled his eyes. "For once in your life, can you stop talking like a stupid pirate? Okay Archie, I'll give it to you. You're no hero. And number two?"

"I stayed home last night and had a movie night with my mom," I said.

Mac's face scrunched up and he snorted in laughter. "Your *mom*? Isn't that precious."

"Arrr," said Barry. "Pirates don't have time for moms."

"Yep, Barry," said McGinley. "Like you said, booger eater. Have fun with the Nimrods, newbie."

I looked to the far corner of the cafeteria. Four boys, the weirdest looking kids in the class. The Nimrods. One of them was drinking his milk through a straw inserted into his nose.

I sat by myself instead.

Chapter Four

I may not have been the type of kid that looked like a hero, but I was. At least, to Mrs. Munderson. She mentioned the incident again the next day in class. How shaken up she had been but how glad she was that there were still people of courage in the world, ready to do the right thing.

That made me feel good.

I sat alone at lunch, and at recess, I sat under a big oak tree, pulled out my comic books, and read.

And that night, as I lay in my bed trying to draw Spiderman and the Green Goblin, I laughed when I realized the only time I'd really been happy since starting school at Kingman was the night I'd put my life in danger to save Mrs. Munderson. Weird, huh?

I went back to reading my comics and drawing when suddenly, it hit me. Maybe I wasn't a hero, but maybe I might just be a super hero. Now, before you laugh, just hear me out. Superheroes like Spiderman and Batman are famous for being loners, struggling with people around them. Maybe, just maybe, that was me? Maybe the cosmos moved my mom and I to crazy California so that it would all become clear?

And what was even weirder, maybe I was actually aware of my own origin story? Whoa. I mean, Spiderman got bit by a radioactive spider. He didn't have any control over what he became. Maybe, just maybe, I was like Batman, except without the millions of dollars, secret cave, and butler.

That was it, I was like Batman. Except, I wasn't Batman.

I saw the newspaper I'd kept on my desk, the one that had the story about Mrs. Munderson. I scrambled over and picked it up and found the section I'd already read over again and again.

When asked to describe the person who saved her, Mrs. Munderson laughed and shook her head.

"I know it sounds crazy," she said, "but the person who saved me was a Pirate Ninja.

I most definitely was *not* Batman.

I was Pirate Ninja.

I stood in front of the mirror. "The name's Ninja," I said to my reflection. "Pirate Ninja." Then I jumped up into the air, attempted a kung fu kick and, instead, landed flat on my back.

It was the worst kung fu kick in history.

And as I stared at the ceiling, it occurred to me that I didn't have a clue how to be a pirate or a ninja. I had a lot of work to do.

Then I smiled. Origin story.

Chapter Five

The next day after school, I rode down to Fisherman's Wharf on the Cove. I figured if I was going to learn about being a pirate, I better start near the water. I spent a half hour walking around, watching guys work on their boats and fishermen going out to sea. And that was when I saw an old, crusty guy with a fake leg.

A fake leg?

That was always the dead giveaway for pirates in the movies and books. I wandered over his way and, as he worked a slipknot on the dock, he grabbed a wooden post and hoisted himself from the boat onto the dock, no problem. When he saw me, his expression changed. He glared at me with mean, crazy eyes. Just like you'd think a pirate would look at you.

And then he said it, those magic words I'd been looking for.

"Arrr, what you looking at, kid?"

Wow, I thought. The cosmos really did want me to be Pirate Ninja.

He growled. "You got sand for brains, kid? I said, what are

you looking at?"

"Um, sorry," I said, "I was just looking for someone."

He looked both ways, then back at me. "I know everybody around here. Who you looking for?"

"Oh," I said, "it's not like that. I'm looking for a certain *kind* of a person."

His face distorted into a confused look. "Are you some kind of weirdo?"

Okay, this may have been a bad idea. I turned to walk away.

"Hold on just a second, kid."

I froze. He was behind me, walking my way, his fake metal leg click-clacking against the dock.

I slowly turned around.

He stood there, mouth twisted up, eyebrows turned down, studying me. I studied him back. His beard was long and scraggly, a perfect mixture of blacks and greys. He had a large, rounded nose. Dark bags hung under his eyes. He wore a fisherman's hat on his head.

"My name's Grievous," he said.

"You're kidding me. Like General Grievous from Star Wars?"

"You really are a weirdo, aren't you, kid?" he said.

"So, you're not the Cyborg supreme commander of the droid army and you don't have four mechanical arms?"

He shook his head, took his cap off and rubbed his head. "When did boys stop playing baseball? No, boy, my name's John Grievous. What's yours?"

"Archie Beller."

"And what type of person are you looking for?" he asked.

"It's hard to explain. You'll think I'm stupid."

"I already think you're stupid," Grievous said. "What have you got to lose?"

I looked around, up one end of the wharf, and down the other. I had to admit, John Grievous here looked like my best chance.

"Well, the truth is…" I hesitated.

"Out with it, boy!"

"I'm looking for a pirate," I spat out.

I didn't think he was expecting that. His eyes got big, and he craned his neck towards me. Then he started laughing. Then he stopped laughing. He looked down at his leg, his fake leg. Then he slowly raised his head. Not laughing anymore. He was serious. Dead serious.

"You trying to be funny, kid?" he practically growled.

I shook my head and backed up. "I'm sorry, really. I'll be going now."

"Stop," he said.

He came close and studied me, then proceeded to walk around like I was undergoing inspection. Then he faced me once again.

"Truth is," he said, "you don't look like some punk. Why are you looking for a pirate?"

I took a deep breath. "I'm trying to learn more about them."

"Why?" he asked.

"Do you know anything about pirates?"

He cocked his head. "A little."

"Really?" I said.

He nodded his head, his gaze still fixed on me.

"Can you tell me what you know?" I said.

"I can, but only if you tell me the real reason you want to know."

"Okay, but you've got to promise not to laugh."

"Archie Beller, the only thing I *can* promise is that I will laugh. But what should you care? I'm just some old guy down at the dock with a fake leg."

A dog barked and a golden retriever raced past me and towards Grievous. The old man bent down and hugged the big dog.

"But I need a refill on coffee first." He pointed behind me, towards a little bait shop. "Keep up."

The dog took off first, and Grievous hobbled by. I followed. Fifty feet later, we came to a medium-sized, wooden building with an old sign over the door that said "Kings Cove Bait Shop." Grievous opened the door and a bell jingled loudly. He walked around the counter and over to a coffee pot. He grabbed a foam cup and poured himself a small cup. He bent down to a mini fridge, grabbed a can of Coke and handed it to me. He sat down on a metal chair at a white table and nodded for me to do the same.

I took a sip of my Coke, then looked around. Old license plates and fishing rods covered the walls. A few empty tins cans as well. "This bait shop is yours?"

He nodded as he took a sip of his coffee. "Ten years now."

"It's really cool," I said.

"Thanks," he said, "but enough with the compliments. Archie Beller, what's the real story here?"

"Do you read the paper?" I asked.

"Every day," he said.

"Did you see the article about Mrs. Munderson, the teacher over at Kingman School?"

He took a slow sip. "The woman who got attacked?" A smile formed on his lips. "And the woman who got saved." He shook his head and laughed. "The newspaper says she got saved by a Pirate Ninja." He pointed his finger at me. "You read about that and now you want to be a Pirate Ninja too, don't you?"

I took another sip of my Coke, then took a long, slow breath. "No Grievous, that's not it at all. You see, well … I *am* the Pirate Ninja."

His eyes popped wide and he leaned in.

"I'm the one who saved Mrs. Munderson," I said.

He narrowed his eyes at me and cocked his head. "Naaah, couldn't be." He sat up straight. "Really?"

I nodded.

"Then how about you tell me exactly what's going on – and don't leave anything out. Got it, Archie?"

So, I told him. I told him everything. When I finished, he rubbed his chin.

"So let me get this straight. You're trying to be some kind of a superhero?"

"Yeah, that's it exactly," I said.

"You know, Archie, you're kind of nuts."

"I am? Yeah, you're right, I totally am," I said.

He waved a hand at me. "You don't understand. Nuts is okay. You can use nuts."

"But can you help me?" I asked.

"Actually," he said, tapping his fingers against the table, "I can. I can, indeed. You're fortunate to have found me."

"I am?"

"Indeed. Listen Archie, tomorrow's Saturday. You doing anything?"

"No," I said.

He stood up. "Good. Then you meet me here at the bait shop. 8am?"

"8am?" I asked.

"Sharp," he said. "And Archie, you better be prepared to work."

Chapter Six

I arrived at the docks at 7:55am the next morning. The sun was still low on the horizon, but shining brightly on the calm waters of the Cove.

"Good," Grievous said as he noticed me. He took a sip of his morning coffee. "You're punctual. That's a start."

I looked around. Two fishermen were climbing out of their boat, and a younger man was dragging an ice chest down the boardwalk. "So, where do we start?"

Grievous held a piece of yellow paper in between his first two fingers. He extended his hand. "We start here," he said.

I grabbed the paper and read. There was a number 1, followed by 'sweep the bait shop.' I looked up but Grievous just stared back.

Next to number 2, it said 'scrub bait shop.' Now I was really confused.

"I don't understand," I said.

"I didn't think you would. It's your training," he said.

"But, sweeping, scrubbing?" I glanced back down at the list. "Hauling out the trash ... what does this have to do with my training?"

"You know, Archie Beller, for a kid who wants help, you sure do ask a lot of questions." He took another long, slow sip and I returned to the list.

"Wait a second," I finally said. "Wait a second. Is this like that movie, *The Karate Kid*? Where Mr. Miagi has the boy do a bunch of chores that end up making him better at karate?"

Grievous smiled and pointed at me. "You're one smart cookie, Archie. I didn't know if you'd seen that movie. Okay then, you'll find the cleaning supplies in the bait shop. You get to work on that list. I'll be working on the boat. That's all."

"That's all?" I said.

"For now," Grievous said.

He turned and hobbled away down the dock and I stepped into the bait shop and went to work. I swept, and then I hit my hands and knees and scrubbed every inch of that floor. I took the trash out to the dumpster and that was when I looked down at my list. Wow, I was barely getting started. Then I remembered *The Karate Kid*. Mr. Miagi had Daniel-san doing work for countless hours to promote muscle memory. I needed to trust that Grievous knew what he was doing.

So I continued working. I tightened the screws on all of the shelving throughout the shop, I cleaned the bathroom in the back, and I unloaded some boxes from a pallet behind the bait shop, and loaded them into the back storage room.

Grievous finally made an appearance, grabbed the list from my hand, and walked around the shop, checking my work. Finally he nodded, pulled a paper bag out of his coat, and handed it to me.

"Fifteen minutes for lunch, then back to the list." He turned the paper around and pointed to the rest of the chores.

So I worked. I worked harder and longer than I'd ever worked in my life and at 5pm that evening, he came back in, checked my work, looked at the list, and nodded his head once again.

"Tomorrow, 8am, sharp," he said.

Then Grievous walked away and back towards his boat.

I was hoping for a little bit more of a personal touch for my pirate and ninja training, but at the moment, I was too tired to care. I rode my bike home, ate whatever my mom put on my plate, went to bed early, and crashed.

The next day, I arrived at 8:15am.

"You're late," Grievous said, taking a sip of his coffee. I swear, all this guy did was sip coffee.

"I had to go to Mass," I said.

"They got church this early?" he said with a confused look.

I nodded.

"Fine," he grumbled. He extended his hand with a new piece of paper. I studied it. Another list, this one longer than the previous day. I took a breath. Just trust the process, I told myself.

And once again, I went to work. After a busy morning, Grievous came in, inspected my work and gave me a lunch. I spent the whole afternoon working in another room filled with junk, off the back end of the bait shot. I moved the junk into a storage garage in the alley behind the shop, then cleaned and scrubbed the entire room out, just like I'd been instructed. By the time the room was empty, cleaned, and scrubbed, I was dragging, both physically and mentally.

"Grievous," I finally said. "Can I ask you a question?"

"Shoot, kid," he said.

"Well, in Karate Kid, Mr. Miagi had Daniel-san do just a few different activities over and over again to build muscle memory. Like paint the fence, sand the floor, those kinds of things. But, you've got me doing such a wide variety of chores. I can't understand how they'll help me."

He smiled. "You *are* one smart cookie indeed, Archie Beller."

"I don't understand," I said.

He scrunched his chin so his lower lip came up over the rest of his mouth. "You got me," he said.

"What do you mean, I got you?" I asked.

"Listen, kid, my shop's coming under inspection by the city next week and frankly, I didn't want to do all the work myself."

"You mean—"

He nodded.

"So this has nothing to do with Karate Kid or Mr. Miagi or my training to be a Pirate Ninja?"

"Nope," he said.

"You lied to me!?" I yelled.

"I thought you wanted to know about pirates. First rule of pirates: they lie to get what they want. You should consider this your first lesson learned."

I could have punched a hole in the wall. "You tricked me into doing all of your work for you?"

"Listen, kid, if you can't spot a trick that obvious, you don't have much chance being a superhero, now do you?"

"You don't know anything about pirates, do you? You don't know anything about ninjas, either. You had no intention of giving me any real training."

"That is where you are wrong," he said.

"Oh wait, I bet you have another list for me, don't you?"

He took a sip. "Follow me, kid."

Grievous hobbled down the dock towards the boat and I stood there watching him. He had lied to me, tricked me into doing his work for him. Why should I follow him?

I gritted my teeth and stomped my foot on the ground.

I was alone in Kings Cove, California surrounded by kids who were obsessed with pirates and ninjas.

Why not follow the one-legged guy down the dock?

Grievous was in his boat by the time I reached him. He extended his hand and I took it. He helped me in. He untied the ropes from the mo0ring posts, then pushed away from the dock and started the motor. He pulled away from the dock and started through the Cove. He motioned for me to join him and I came alongside. Grievous nodded, but said nothing, just kept navigating the boat and pulling further away from shore. Finally, he cut the engine.

"Okay, Archie. To be a pirate, you gotta know about boats and the sea. First off, how far would you say we are from shore?"

I shrugged. "Half a mile, maybe?"

"I'd say more like three quarters of a mile. Judging distance on the sea is difficult but vitally important. Next, you need to know the different parts of the boat. Think about the boat being split up into thirds for ease. The third closest to the front of the boat is called the forward part of the boat, and the tip of the front of the boat is called the bow. The middle third is called amidships and the back third is called the aft."

We walked to the aft and he pointed down to the very back of the boat. "This here is called the stem. Go ahead, take a good look." He leaned over and I did, too. When I did, he pushed me hard, and I fell headfirst into the ocean water. I screamed and then I looked up.

"What the heck?" I yelled, then promptly swallowed a mouthful of water.

He nodded. "Good, you can swim."

I spit and coughed. "Good, I can swim? Are you crazy?" I screamed.

"Now let's see how well you can swim. Like I said, it's about three quarters of a mile back to shore. I'll meet you at the bait shop."

"What?! No! You can't do this," I yelled.

But Grievous was back up to the forward part of the boat, pulling the boat away. I treaded water as he swung the boat around in a big U-turn and headed back towards the docks.

I was alone, completely. I was in the ocean, and this maniac wanted me to swim longer than I'd ever swam before in my life.

I had two choices: stop swimming or swim.

Okay, well, I really only had one choice.

I swam, sucking up tons of water as I went. Swimming in the ocean was an entirely different experience than swimming in the pools and lakes around Omaha. Salt water splashed into my eyes, mouth, and nose and I had to stop every twenty feet to cough and regain my breath and composure. But then I would take a look at the shore, the shore that looked so far away, and know that if I didn't get going I would never, ever make it.

Not making it wasn't a good option.

So I swam. I had no idea how long it took and there were several more moments when I thought about giving up, but I didn't. And when I made it to the docks, several fishermen looked at me weird as I continued to swim towards shore. Finally, I got close enough to where I could touch and I slowly crawled the rest of the way out of the water, on my hands and knees, coughing and spitting out salt water.

I looked towards the bait shop. Grievous relaxed out front in a chair, sipping coffee, looking as happy as could be.

I lost it. I jumped from the docks onto the boardwalk, and stomped over there.

"What do you think you're doing?" I yelled.

"Just enjoying my coffee. Good job making it back to

shore, Archie."

"You're crazy! I could have died! I've never swum in the ocean. I've never swam that far in my life!"

"But you made it all the same, didn't you?" he said without any trace of humor.

I pointed at him. "You … you don't know the first thing about pirates or ninjas or helping me. You're just a twisted old dude, aren't you? You're a fake!"

Grievous dumped his coffee over and stood right up. His right fist clenched into a ball, and then relaxed.

"You don't know anything about pirates and ninjas," I repeated.

"No, Archie, I do not," he said, teeth together, jaw twitching.

"Then I'm outta here," I said.

"Stop," he said forcefully.

"Why should I?" I said. "Oh, I know. So you make me do all your chores and practically kill me, right?"

"Are you done?" Grievous said, his voice strong and steady. "Okay, Archie, it's true. I don't know anything about pirates and ninjas. I can't teach you how to say 'Ahoy,' or search for treasure, or do kung fu. But if you want to learn about the sea, about boats, and about fighting? I can help you out. My name is Grievous. I may not be a Cyborg Star Wars leader, but in my former life, I was Naval Commander John Grievous. Before this…" He pointed to his fake leg. "I was a Navy Seal. Navy Seals know more about the water than a pirate ever could, and they know more about fighting than ninjas ever did. I made you do those stupid chores to see if you would follow my orders. I dropped you off in the water so you could prove to yourself you could do something hard. No more dumb chores, I promise, but if you're willing to come by after school and on the weekends, I'll train you. I'll train you hard. I'll teach you everything you need to know."

"To be a Pirate Ninja?" I asked.

"To be *the* Pirate Ninja," he said.

Chapter Seven

The weekend of chores had just about done me in, and I found myself dragging through school the next day. As usual, the pirates and ninjas avoided me, and I spent recess reading comic books under the oak tree. After school, I rode my bike down to the Cove and found Grievous sitting in front of his bait shop.

"You ever heard of a burpee?" Grievous asked without even saying hi.

I scratched my chin. "Is that when you belch after drinking a Slurpee?"

Grievous mumbled something under his breath, then climbed down off the boardwalk and walked to the middle of the beach. "The burpee will be the core of your physical fitness training. They're hard, but after a while you will learn—"

"To love them?" I interrupted.

He made a face. "No, heck no. You'll hate 'em. You never learn to love them. But, you will learn how to do lots of something you hate, and if you want to be *the* Pirate Ninja, then that's what you'll have to do. Are you ready?"

I nodded.

Grievous bent down into a squat position. "Okay, sailor, from the squat position, you lower to the ground through a squat thrust like this." He lowered to the ground and kicked his feet out at the same time. I was surprised by how well he could move and how well he could throw his fake leg back.

"Now, you do a pushup." He did a strong, controlled pushup, suddenly looking much younger than his long gray beard suggested.

"Now you do a frog jump, like this." He shot his legs forward so that he was in a squatting position again.

"And lastly, you finish with a jump squat." He jumped into the air, and landed a little unevenly. "Got it?" he asked.

"No," I said.

He smiled. "Great, now get in position."

I did burpees for the next hour. By the end, I fell like throwing up. I asked for water, and he gave me a small Styrofoam cup only half full.

"Good," he said. "Now you should be warmed up."

"Warmed up?" I said, my voice cracking more than a little.

"Into the water, sailor," he said.

Without a doubt, the three hours I spent with Grievous that afternoon were the worst three hours of my life. When 6:30 rolled around and he blew a whistle, I fell into the sand. He walked past me and towards the bait shop.

"See you tomorrow, Archie," was all he said. I think he really enjoyed seeing me in pain.

I limped back to the docks every afternoon that week, and each evening at 6:30 I fell into a heap, promising myself I would never go back. And each day, I did. On Saturday, I arrived at 8am sharp.

Grievous was eating a donut from a large white box. He looked my way. "Want one, Archie?"

Boy, did I ever. All the crazy physical conditioning had ramped my appetite through the roof and Mom hadn't been able to keep enough food in the house for me.

"Thanks, Grievous," I said as I reached for one. He knocked my hand away. "I didn't say you get one. I just asked if you wanted one."

"But, I thought—"

"Yeah, I don't care what you thought. But, I will give you a chance to *win* these donuts."

"Win them?" I asked, more than a little deflated.

Grievous winked. "Follow me."

He walked around to the back of his bait shop and opened it up. We were in the large back room he'd had me clear out and clean. It looked a lot different now. There was a blue wrestling mat covering the floor, and a large punching bag hanging from the ceiling in the corner.

"Wow," I said.

"Archie, you've done well with the physical fitness. You're tough, and you don't give up. Now it's time you learn how to fight."

Grievous went to the corner and picked up what looked like a long, brown sword. He threw it to me and I caught it with two hands. It was made completely out of wood.

"It's a training sword," he said. "Here's the deal: you beat me, you get those donuts."

"And how do I beat you?"

He grinned. "You'll know when you beat me."

I grabbed the sword and held it like I thought somebody should hold a sword, then I met Grievous in the middle of the room.

"But you're not holding a sword," I said.

"No offense, kid, but I won't be needing one against you."

I looked at him again. He was old and he had a fake leg. What did he mean?

"Archie, on the count of three, I want you to try and kill me."

"Kill you?"

He nodded. "Okay, one, two, three, go!"

I came at him fast, and like a blur, he spun away and kicked me in the side with his fake leg. I shot through the air and landed four feet away. I held my ribs where he'd gotten me. I looked up.

"You can do better than that, can't you?" he asked.

I stumbled to my feet and came at him again, and again, and again. Each time with a similarly terrible result. Not only could I not hit the one-legged old man, he was beating the stuffing out of me too. After thirty minutes, I was drenched in a pool of sweat, my hands on my knees, trying to regain my breath.

"How do you do that?" I finally said.

"A lot of practice," he said.

"Can you teach me?" I said.

He smirked. "You know, you could've avoided a lot of pain had you asked me that twenty minutes ago."

Grievous grabbed my fake sword and threw it to the side, and then he started to teach. He said that in the military, you used the very best of all the different martial arts and wrestling techniques, kind of like they do in mixed martial arts. He explained that real fights are down and dirty. There are no rules, and you've got to get in and get out as quickly as you can.

We worked all morning. At lunch, he threw me a paper bag. "Not here," he said. "Now we head back to the boat."

"And are you going to throw me off the side again?"

"First of all, I threw you off the aft. And second of all, yeah, probably."

I ate my lunch while Grievous pulled the boat away from the docks and into the Cove. Very quickly, we were out of the Cove and into the real ocean. I looked back to the shore, watching it fade away in the distance. I really hoped he didn't throw me overboard from here.

And that's precisely when he pushed me and yes, I fell overboard and into the water.

He looked down at me, grinning. "Now Archie, don't freak out. Worst thing you can do in water is freak out. I'm not gonna make you swim back to shore. It's time to work on your strength." He threw a rope ladder overboard. "Grabbing a rope ladder from the water and pulling yourself up is approximately a hundred times harder than it looks, but it's something a SEAL has to be proficient at. Ready to begin?"

I swam for the ladder, the boat rocking and pulling away from me as I made the first lunge for the rope rungs. I swallowed a huge mouthful of saltwater instead.

He was right; it wasn't easy.

I buried my head in the water and swam for the boat again. I got closer this time, then grabbed onto the rope ladder. That was when I realized what Grievous was talking about. I tried to pull myself up while the boat rocked and swayed on the ocean waves. I tried to gather my legs below me and did, for a moment – just enough to reach for the next rung on the ladder. But then my grip gave way and I fell back into the water.

I looked up and Grievous was grinning, holding up a large donut with white frosting.

"Listen, Archie, I'll sweeten the pot here a little. You make it up that ladder, and you get this beautiful donut. You don't even have to beat me up."

I didn't make it up the ladder that afternoon, but I did get close.

So as a consolation prize, Grievous threw the donut into the water and I had to retrieve it. No matter what you might be thinking, wet donuts really aren't that great. But they're better than nothing, so I took it.

We kept at the training. Every day I would manage my invisible, lonely existence at school, and every afternoon I would ride down to the Cove and train with Grievous. Then on the weekends, nothing but training. You would think my mom would mind me being gone all the time, but she had enough to worry about with her own job. Plus, she was happy that I was keeping busy. Anyways, I kept this crazy training schedule up for the next month and then, at 6:15 on a Friday evening, Grievous blew his whistle early.

"What's wrong?" I asked.

"Nothing, Archie, nothing at all. Listen, you've done a great job and I'm really, really—well, you've done a great job. I gotta leave town for a couple weeks, head back east and take care of some things, so you'll have to do your training without me."

"Really?" I said, not able to hide my disappointment.

"Yeah, but I got something for you." He pointed to a box over in the corner. It was wrapped in newspapers. Don't open it until you're at home and away from your mom, got it?"

"Yeah, sure thing. Thanks, Grievous."

"And one more thing, I think it's time you try for those dry donuts again." He walked over and grabbed a white box from underneath a sweatshirt. He opened it up. Six hot glazed, six cake with white frosting. Man, they smelled good.

Grievous grabbed the fake wooden sword and threw it my way. I snatched it out of the air. But this time, he grabbed one himself. He tossed it from one hand to the other.

"But I've never fought you when you've been armed before," I said.

"Well, boy, it's about time you do. One, two, three. Go!"

I didn't come right at him this time. One thing Grievous had taught me was patience. Getting in fast and closing hard was ideal, but it didn't always work. Against a skilled opponent, counterattack was one of the best methods, one Grievous had been drilling me on for weeks.

After dancing around each other for a couple minutes, Grievous finally came at me swinging. But I blocked with my sword, ducked, and swept my foot along the floor in an arc. Grievous hopped over it with his one good leg, then counterattacked with a large left cut of his sword, like he was trying to hit a home run out of the park. I ducked under that one, rolled, and countered.

We went back and forth like this for the next few minutes. My body was fatiguing and, I think his was, as well. I needed to change the status quo and give myself an advantage. I noticed the light hanging down from the middle of the room. The only light in the room.

It was a truly stupid idea. And that meant it might just work.

I rolled to my left, kicked at his knee, and he jumped back. Then, I coiled my sword back, but instead of attacking him, I flicked my wrist, released my weapon, and watched it sail over him and destroy the light above his head. His head swung towards the blown out light just like I'd hoped, and before he knew what hit him, I ran at him, slid on my knees, punched him where it hurt and slid through his legs. He crumpled to the ground as I picked up my sword and jumped onto his chest. I whacked him in the chest twice with the end of my wooden sword. Then he yelled, "STOP!"

He got up slowly, moaning, coughing, and rubbing his chest, and that other area. Then he looked at me and forced a smile. "Looks like you just won yourself some donuts."

Chapter Eight

After gorging myself on frozen pizza that night, I retired to my room and locked the door. I grabbed Grievous's present off the desk, and started ripping away the newspaper wrapping paper. I took the lid off the large white rectangular box and, for a moment, lost my breath.

It was black, grey, and red. I pulled it out of the box and held it up. Wow. It was a Pirate Ninja suit and about a million times better than that thrown together costume I had worn the night I'd saved Munderson. I stepped into it, pulled it up, ran the zipper up the front and did the latches. I pulled the ninja hood over my head and when I looked into the mirror noticed that a red pirate bandana was attached to it. There, in the box, I spotted another accessory. An eye patch. I carefully attached it around my head and adjusted it so that it fit tight. Then I noticed, the eye patch only looked black. It was tinted. I could see out of it just fine.

I returned to the mirror and checked out my suit.

It. Looked. So. AWESOME! And, it felt awesome. The suit fit perfectly, like it was tailored to fit me. There was thick material across my chest, arms, ribs, and thighs, as if to protect me from body blows.

In the gift box was something else, a wooden sword. Around the waist was a utility belt. I unsnapped the cover. Whoa!

There was a grappling hook, a set of screwdrivers and pliers, and a small pair of binoculars.

Grievous was not messing around.

I returned to the mirror and checked myself out. No doubt about it.

I *was* Pirate Ninja.

I noticed a yellow note in the box and grabbed it.

"Archie, I may not be a pirate or a ninja, but I'm a Navy Seal and that's the closest the world will get to a real Pirate Ninja. Until now. From one Pirate Ninja to another, you, Archie Beller, are ready. Time to ride."

Time to ride?

A chill ran down my spine. That's what I had done all this training for: to help the Mrs. Mundersons of the world, to fight crime, to be a super hero.

And after all the training, I was ready. Grievous was right. It was definitely time to ride.

I opened my door a crack and asked Mom if I could meet some friends at the movie theater. She shouted 'hooray' from the bathroom, and told me to have fun. I snuck out the back, left the house, and hopped on my bike.

I rode downtown, sticking to the side streets and alleys. I figured if someone needed the help of Pirate Ninja, it would be somewhere in the shadows and dark places of Kings Cove.

As the cool evening air rushed through the eyeholes of my ninja mask, I thought about what I was doing. I was a 5th grader, riding my bike down dark alleys on a Friday Night, looking for trouble. Yep, I was basically insane.

And, after a while, I realized that I was also basically bored. Apparently, the criminals of Kings Cove got the memo that Pirate Ninja was on patrol because things were slow and quiet, and I was growing anxious. And then, just when I thought I might just fall asleep and fall off my bike, a cat meowed and I jumped. Then the big black cat saw me, startled, and ran down the alley. That was when I heard something else. Something human.

Voices. Loud voices. Shouting, actually. Coming from the end of the alley.

I slowed my bike, and listened more intently. Two voices, both shouting. A terrible argument. Could be nothing, of course – people argue all the time. I leaned my bike against the brick wall of an old building and tiptoed forward, trying to be as quiet as possible. The voices rose and I stopped.

"Don't!" shouted one of the voices.

This wasn't nothing. There was panic in that voice. Something terrible was definitely happening. I took a deep breath. This was what all the training was for.

I *was* Pirate Ninja and *this* was my moment.

I pulled my wooden sword from its sheath, and walked quickly and quietly towards the noise.

Light poured out onto the alley from an open door. The voices were coming from that open door, from inside the building. The shouting grew in intensity.

"Don't, don't kill me!" the voice practically screamed.

Kill? I swallowed hard. I couldn't back down, not now. Someone inside that building was in the worst kind of trouble, and I, Pirate Ninja, was the only one who could help. I closed my eyes, took one last breath, made the sign of the cross, and gripped my sword.

"Please," the voice begged. I burst through the door and sprinted towards the noise. I moved down a hall with racks of clothes on both sides and made a left at a dead end. I saw a scary dude with long hair and weird clothes holding his sword, reading to attack a woman on the floor.

Now was my time. I sprang into action, rolled onto the floor and before he knew what hit him, came up with my sword and hit the attacker hard across the knuckles. He dropped his sword, and howled in pain. I followed that by sweeping his feet with mine. He fell backwards, and then I hopped onto his chest and held my wooden sword against his head. I turned slightly behind me and looked as a woman stood there with a horrified expression.

"Are you okay, ma'am?" I asked.

She covered her face in horror, clearly in too much shock to move. I returned my gaze to the villain at the end of my sword.

"You either leave and never come back," I said, "or I'll be forced to call the police—or worse." I growled in order to make it extra scary.

"Dude," the man gurgled. "We're in the middle of a play."

"I don't want your flimsy excuses," I said. "Your wrath of terror is done. You hear me? Done!"

He extended his finger and pointed to the side. "No, you idiot," he said. "We're performing—a play."

I suddenly had a very, very bad feeling. I slowly turned my head to the side and watched as a large room full of eyes stared back at me.

A play.

Oh, no!

I lifted my foot off the man's chest, but it was too late. Security guards were running down the aisles of the theatre towards the stage. I heard noise behind me. Even more guards came at me from the opposite direction.

I could just tell them the truth, that I'd made a terrible mistake. But then everyone would know my identity. And that meant the thug who attacked Munderson would know my identity.

I couldn't let that happen.

The security guards were closing in and I needed to act. I

needed to act like a ninja—Pirate Ninja.

I put the sword in its sheath, and sprinted for the nearest stage curtain. I grabbed hold of it with two hands and started climbing up that curtain. The last month of training had made climbing a piece of cake, and this curtain was no exception. When I reached the top of the curtain, I lunged for a metal beam that ran across the top of the stage and held various lights and ropes. When I grabbed it, the entire audience gasped. I shimmied along it until I was in position, then hung with one hand—monkey bars style—while I reached with the other hand and found what I was looking for. A rope. I untied that rope with one hand and then, when I thought it would work, swallowed hard and grabbed the rope with both hands. I let go. I immediately dropped ten feet straight down and just barely kept grip on the rope when it started to swing away from me and towards the main stage below. Security guards were communicating via walkie-talkies, when all of a sudden they realized what was happening—that I was coming straight for them!

The guards dove away at the last minute and it was like I was a bowling ball and they were the pins. I picked up major speed, and let go at the last possible moment, flying headfirst into the stage curtain at the back of the stage. I landed against the ground with a thud, but didn't have time to think or worry about it.

I scrambled to my feet, and ran through the hallways, toppling over the racks of clothes as I sprinted past. I bolted through the door and into the back alley, then sprinted to my bike, hopped on and never, ever looked back.

Twenty minutes later, I stopped in my driveway, threw my bike down and slipped into the house. Mom was asleep in her favorite chair so I slipped past, went into my room, locked the door and collapsed onto my bed.

I was an idiot, a complete fool. And, as I buried my head into my pillow, I knew that just as soon as it had begun, Pirate Ninja was over.

Chapter Nine

I was hoping the hundreds of people at the Orpheum Theatre who'd witnessed me act like an insane moron the night before might sort of forget about what they'd seen.

I was wrong.

When I arrived at Mrs. Munderson's class the next morning, kids were huddled around McGinley while Munderson was at her desk, staring out the window. I walked around and looked at the paper—at the headline on the front page:

Pirate Ninja Strikes Again

What?

I sat and tried to calm myself down but McGinley was rustling the stupid paper and laughing.

"Oh man," he said. "You guys gotta listen to this:

Police are now formulating a new character sketch of the figure known as Pirate Ninja. According to Detective Norm Peterson, 'We now believe that Pirate Ninja is some sort of unstable sociopath. We think his intervention in the purse snatching was purely accidental, that what he was truly after was a fight.' When Detective Peterson was asked if Pirate Ninja was now being considered a criminal, Peterson paused. 'Let's just say, we want Pirate Ninja off the streets as quickly as possible.'"

McGinley set down his paper and said, "Sounds like your superhero isn't such a hero after all, eh, Mrs. Munderson?"

Mrs. Munderson shook her head, then stood up. "That's enough Mr. McGinley. Put the papers away and let's begin."

Well, that wasn't enough, not by a long shot. Pirate Ninja, criminal number one, was all anybody could talk about all morning. At recess, I noticed McGinley and the ninjas weren't practicing their kung fu grips for a change. Instead, they were huddled together in deep conversation.

I wanted to know what they were talking about so I quietly tiptoed behind them, crouched down, and listened. As usual, it was McGinley talking.

"Think about it, dudes," he said. "What better way to prove our ninja cred to the world than to find and capture this Pirate Ninja psycho?"

"Where would we even find him?" one of the others asked.

"We know from the paper that he was cruising the alleys down by the Orpheum Theatre. I say we hide in those areas ninja-style and when Pirate Ninja comes by, we get him."

"You really think we can?" asked Mike.

McGinley punched his hand with his fist. "I know we can. Tonight will be the last night Pirate Ninja walks the streets of Kings Cove."

"What?" I said. Oops. I'd meant to say that in my head. The entire group of ninjas turned towards me. McGinley squeezed through and got in my face.

"Are you spying on us Archie?"

"No, I um, I just heard you talking about that crazy Pirate Ninja guy."

"I'm pretty sure you're not welcome here. You had your chance. Now beat it."

"Listen, Mac," I said. "You can't go after that guy. You're just a bunch of kids. You'll get hurt."

"Ha!" he said. "We're not just kids, we're ninjas. And since when are you so interested in what we do, anyway?"

"Um, no reason," I said. "I just don't want to see a fellow—um, what *is* our school's mascot anyway?"

"We're the Mud Floppers, moron. Don't you know anything?"

"Well," I said. "I know I don't want to see a fellow Mud Flopper get hurt by this psycho, okay?"

McGinley rolled his eyes. "Touching, really. But we're not going after Pirate Ninja as Mud Floppers—we're going after him as ninjas. And when we're done with him, this town's gonna realize who the real heroes are around here." He stuck his finger in my chest and jabbed it hard. "So back off Archie from Omaha, and keep your nose out of our business. You had your chance, and you blew it."

McGinley glared at me, then backed away, and he and his ninjas went back to practicing their flying front kicks. I walked away, and found my large oak tree. I sat at the bottom of it and leaned against the trunk.

What on earth was I going to do?

"Ahhhhh!" someone yelled from above me as a figure came flying through the tree and landed five feet in front of me.

I stumbled to my feet. "What the heck!" I said.

To my left and to my right, figures appeared. And then a fourth came around the tree and joined the figure that had jumped down off the tree.

I looked at them all. It wasn't the ninjas and it wasn't the pirates. A tall boy stepped forward. He had humongous ears, big teeth, and glasses the size of dinner plates.

"That's right, Archie," he said in a nasally voice. "The Nimrods."

"W-what are you guys doing?"

"Frankly, Archie, we're tired of waiting. You had enough sense to refuse the invitation of those loser ninjas and pirates, and we thought that meant we'd be getting a fifth member soon. But days, weeks, and months have gone by, and yet you choose to remain alone. Explain yourself."

"What do you mean, explain myself?" I said.

The tall kid shook his head like he was disappointed in me. "Are we really that horrible, that's it better to be alone than to be seen with us? Really?"

"Well, I, um … Well, to be honest, the other guys said you're a bunch of booger eaters."

All four boys exchanged knowing looks. The tall kid folded his arms and glared at me. "For your information, Freddy's the only one among us who is *still* a booger eater."

The figure to my left stuck his index finger into his nose,

pulled out a green one, and stuck it in his mouth. "I can't help it," he said, "they're just so tasty."

"That's gross!" I said.

"Yes it is, Archie," said the tall kid ,"but Freddy's our friend and we stick by him, booger eater or not."

"And well, the guys … they also call you the Nimrods," I said.

"Well, for your information," said the tall kid, "we came up with that name first."

"But why? Why on earth would you call yourself Nimrods? You do realize they're calling you dumb and dimwitted, right?"

The tall kid snort-laughed, and pushed his glasses against his nose with his fingers. "Well, the joke's on those idiots. Nimrod was a fearsome warrior in the Bible and we're named after him."

Seriously?

"But I don't think anybody in the world knows that except for you," I said.

"Not our fault that they're the dimwitted ones, now is it?" The tall kid snort-laughed again and high-fived Freddy.

"Okay," I said, "but what do you want from me?"

"Simple. We're offering you protection. We're offering you friendship and we're offering you a life of not being alone."

"I'm sorry…?"

"Eduardo. My name's Eduardo."

"I'm sorry, Eduardo, but I've got a lot on my mind right

now."

"And if you were our friend, you could tell us about it," he said.

"I'm sorry, I can't," I said.

"Then I'm disappointed in you, Archie," said Eduardo. "We were hoping you might be different. You *are* from Nebraska, after all. Come on boys, let's ride."

Eduardo sneered at me, then motioned with his hand. All four Nimrods skipped back to their light pole.

And I was truly alone.

Chapter Ten

I really wished Grievous hadn't left town. He was the only person I could discuss this with. Heck, he might even been able to help me figure out what to do. I thought about my options. I could always tell my mom. She would completely freak out and the two of us would probably be in another state by the next morning. That wouldn't work. I could go to the police. Scratch that. The police were looking for me; I couldn't go to them. Nope, the more I thought about it, the more I knew there was only one option that made any sense. If I was going to make sure Mac and the ninjas stayed out of serious trouble, I was going to have to take care of this by myself.

I told my mom that a group of kids had invited me over to their house and once again, she was thrilled. She hugged me close. "I think California is our pot of gold, Archie. Yes, buddy, our pot of gold."

I suited up, waited until Mom was in the bathroom, hollered goodbye, and snuck out of the house. I rode my bike towards downtown and once I got close, ditched it behind a bush, and traveled the rest of the way on foot.

If there were ninjas lurking in the shadows, I would need to get some place where I could keep an eye on them. I snuck behind cars, zigzagged in between buildings, and sprinted down alleys until I got close to the part of town where the Orpheum theatre sat, and where I'd made a fool of myself just a day before.

I looked up and found what I was looking for. An old, rusted out fire escape about twenty feet above me. I dug my toes into the brick façade of the old building, and climbed straight up. I lunged for the metal fire escape, grabbed on and pulled myself up. I tiptoed all the way up the fire escape and then climbed the last ten feet until I made it to the roof of the four-story building.

From this height, I had a great view of the city. The moon was full, and lit up the night. The moonlight danced off the waters of the Cove and down below, the city bustled.

And somewhere, amidst all of it, a group of fifth grade ninjas lay in wait. I'd noticed before that many of the rooftops in this section of downtown connected and I figured I could monitor most of the activities from my perch up here.

Now it was time to wait and watch.

It didn't take too long. Fifteen minutes later, I saw four ninjas enter the alley below me, like large rats scurrying about. They stuck to the edges of the walls, hiding behind enormous black trash bags and green metal dumpsters. I had to give it to McGinley: he and his ninjas were committed. But there had to be more than four. I ran silently to the other end of the roof and spotted half a dozen more ninjas spreading out through two other alleys. I hopped down to the rooftop of the building next door and kept scanning below. I spotted the remaining ten ninjas: five coming from one direction, five coming from another. All in all, it looked like they were monitoring four different alleys, waiting for Pirate Ninja. Little did they know, I was above them, studying their every move.

Turns out, when ninjas are hiding in the darkness, they're boring. Super boring. Over the next hour and a half, they just sat there in silence. I had to admit, I was more than a little impressed with their dedication. But I was also hoping they would get tired and move on.

But they didn't move on. I was bored *and* I was beginning to dread the thought that McGinley might bring his fellow ninjas back night after night until they accomplished their mission.

That was when I saw one of the ninjas jump, just as I heard the sound of metal clanking against metal. I turned towards my right and looked down. A big guy was pushing a small man out of the door and into the alley. The small man fell backwards and landed on his back. The big guy stepped over him and shook his fist.

That big guy seemed familiar.

"You double-crossed me, Micky," he said. That was when I knew. The guy was definitely familiar. He was the thug who'd attacked Mrs. Munderson. The one who said he'd get me once he found out who I was.

I swallowed hard, then remembered the words of Navy

SEAL John Grievous. I was ready for this. Plus, I'd faced this thug once before and won. I could do it again.

I inched along the roof so I could get closer. I looked below. Part of me wanted to jump down there and stop him, and help that poor guy. But then I remembered the ninjas. At least half a dozen, hidden in that alley, waiting for me.

I couldn't risk it. Not yet.

That's when I heard it. To my left, footsteps, like someone running. I swung my head and watched as a ninja sprinted in at top speed. Then he yelled. "Ninja Power!"

Oh, no. McGinley. What an idiot!

That must have been some kind of signal because of all a sudden, fifth grade ninjas were coming towards the two men from every direction.

The thug yelled out, "Boys, we got trouble!" The door clanked as three more large men ran out into the alley.

Uh oh.

A group of fifth grade ninjas against four very large – and my guess was, very tough – criminals.

This was a recipe for disaster. I thought again about calling the police but it was too late for that.

McGinley screamed again and went right at the group of thugs. My old mugger friend stuck his boot out, caught McGinley in the chest, and sent the poor kid flying back and to the side where he crashed into a trash can.

I thought that might be enough to send the other ninjas running away. It wasn't. They all charged at once, and, one by one, the four big dudes kicked, punched and threw those ninjas back like they were fifth graders.

Which, of course, they were.

I was out of time. I needed to stop watching and start acting.

I opened up the tool belt and yanked out the grappling hook. I pulled it out as far as it would go. I tossed it across to the building on the other side of the alley and was lucky enough that it caught on a fire escape on that side. I pulled the rope tight, made the sign of the cross, and I jumped, just like I had at the theatre. I swung down fast and hard, and before I started swinging to the other side, I dropped.

It all happened way too fast for those big dudes. I kicked the first in the head just as he looked up. He crumpled into a heap as I landed on him and rolled off.

I pulled my wooden sword out and swept the legs of the next dude before he knew what I'd done. I followed up with two quick shots to the stomach that knocked the wind out of him.

That gave the other two dudes enough time to get their

bearings.

And there was my old friend.

He pointed at me. "You!" he roared. "So, Pirate Ninja comes to save the day, eh? Well, today you won't be so lucky. Get 'em, Dino!"

The two of them rushed me at the same time, from two different directions. I immediately turned and burst towards the brick building no more than eight feet away. I jumped up, hit my right foot against the wall, climbed up with my left foot and pushed off with the most violent force I could muster. I did a backwards somersault and by some freakish miracle, landed on my feet. I swung my wooden sword hard and nailed Dino in the kidneys. He dropped to his knees and howled in pain. But my mugger friend regrouped quickly. He let loose with a spinning backhand fist that nailed me in the chest, sending me backwards. I flew until I landed on my butt. Thank goodness Grievous had put in some extra padding in the suit.

The thug was standing over me, picking his boot up, ready to drive it down hard on my chest. I spun just in time to miss him, then drove my wooden sword into the side of his knee. He screamed in pain, and as he did, I hit him with one shot in his lower back, then followed up with a shot to the gut. He crumpled over.

All four dudes lay in the alley, moaning and writhing in pain. And in the middle was the small man who had been attacked in the first place. I'd almost forgotten about him. I went to him, and helped him up.

"Who, who are you?" he asked, trembling.

I shook my head and pointed down the alley. Then I pushed him and growled in a low voice. "Go."

He stumbled at first, and then took off running down the alley. I picked up my sword and advanced over one of the big dudes in a threatening way. He held his hand up and shook his head. Then he got to his feet and helped the other three up. The mugger wanted to come back for me but one of his friends pulled him away. They started running the opposite way but the mugger stopped and screamed from the end of the alley. "This isn't over, Pirate Ninja. This will never be over!"

Quickly, the four goons were gone, and I took a deep breath. That was close. Too close.

But I didn't have time to rest. The hair stood up on the back of my neck and I turned. A group of fifth grade ninjas stood there, staring at me. I got the tingly feeling again, and spun to the other side. Another group of ninjas stared at me.

"So," McGinley said. "If it isn't the psychopath who calls himself Pirate Ninja."

Oh no. I wanted to say something, to tell him I'd just saved his life, but I knew I couldn't say anything. Mac had talked to me too many times. Even if I disguised my voice, there was too much risk in talking. He'd know it was me.

He carefully stepped my way.

"You may have gotten lucky with those four guys," he said, "but let's see how you do against twenty ninjas."

He was right. Even though I was way better than them,

there were just too many. They would overwhelm me. I had to do something.

"Cat got your Pirate Ninja tongue?" he said like the total jerk he was.

I looked around for some kind of way out. They were practically everywhere and I had only one option.

"Okay, boys, get him!" he yelled.

Ninja screams filled the alley as they charged at me from both sides. I darted to my right and back to my trusty brick wall. As I leapt against it one more time, I heard the sound of twenty ninjas crashing into each other behind me. I pushed off the wall violently with my left foot, then spun backwards into a somersault. This time I landed on top of a huge pile of fifth graders. I got my balance and looked straight up at the grappling line still dangling from where I'd left it. With one giant leap, I lunged for it and caught it with two hands. I immediately started swinging my body and the line swung with me. I needed momentum.

Below me, ninjas jumped up and swiped at me. I pulled my feet up as I swung. Finally, I built up enough momentum to where I landed against the opposite wall, then shoved off and went backwards. *Okay feet*, I thought, *don't fail me now.* I came back towards the brick wall, but this time when I hit it I quickly ran up the side, and climbed the rope at the same time. When I reached as high as I could, I leapt from the rope and grabbed onto the bottom rung of the fire escape.

I pulled myself up and over that rung. And then looked down at the ninjas below.

They were screaming at me.

I smiled but they would never know it because of my ninja hood. Then, I saluted them, turned around, and ran up the fire escape as fast as I could. When I reached the rooftop, I sprinted and jumped from rooftop to rooftop until I was more than a block away. Eventually, I climbed down from a building, found the bush where I'd stashed my bike, then climbed aboard and rode off into the black night.

On the ride home, I finally took a breath and reflected on what had happened. All in all, not bad. Pirate Ninja had managed to save an innocent man, fight off a group of criminals, and save his fellow Mud Sloppers in the process.

Not bad at all.

Chapter Eleven

I noticed McGinley and the other ninjas walking around a little more slowly than usual at school the next day. Barry and the pirates growled at them and said they looked like a bunch of yellow-bellied, old geezers, whatever that meant.

Meanwhile, I had made a decision. Being a Pirate Ninja was great and all, but after last night, I was tired of it being all about me against the world. I needed more than my mom and an old bearded guy named Grievous. I needed friends. Especially now that I understood hanging with the pirates and the ninjas was never ever going to happen.

And since fifth grade boys don't hang out with girls—that left only one group.

And so, I grabbed my lunch and found their table in the corner. I walked up and Eduardo hit Freddy and pointed my direction.

"So, guys," I said. "Any chance you'd let me eat lunch with you?"

Eduardo folded his arms and twisted his mouth up into an awfully weird face. Freddy, of course, picked his nose.

Finally, Eduardo's face relaxed into a smile.

"Ahhh, of course Archie, sit down and meet everybody."

I sat down at the end of the table. Eduardo and Freddy were on my right. On my left, a heavy kid with enormous eyes and a small nose smiled so wide, I thought the smile might wrap around the back of his head. "The name's Norman," he said. The kid next to him was short with a head the size of a bb pellet. Okay, exaggeration, but only a little. He grinned, too. "My name's Quentin."

"Cool," I said. "So, Eduardo, Freddy, Norman, and Quentin, nice to meet you guys. As you know, my name's Archie and, well, first off, is there any chance you guys might reconsider the whole Nimrods name?"

Eduardo and the others exchanged a funny look. "No chance, Archie. We've got a logo and everything. Even working on a website, right Quentin?"

Quentin nodded.

"A logo?" I said.

"And a website," Quentin said.

"Yeah," said Eduardo, "plus who cares about our name? We need to get down to serious business."

"Really?" I said. "What kind of serious business?"

"Well, for starters," said Eduardo, "we need to know who your favorite super hero is?"

My heart skipped a beat. "D-did you just say superhero?"

"Yeah," said Freddy. "We're not into ninjas and pirates like the rest of the freaks at this school." He wiped a booger on the table. "We're normal. We like superheroes."

The Nimrods wanted to know my favorite superhero?

Maybe California wasn't a complete disaster, after all.

"And Archie," said Eduardo, "I swear, if you say something lame like Superman, I'll let Freddy flick a booger at you."

I started to say something, when Eduardo held up a finger. "And Batman's really not that cool either, so tread carefully here."

I leaned in. "Have any of you guys ever heard of the Black Panther?"

Eduardo looked over at Freddy and the two of them high-fived.

"As in T'Challa, King of Wakanda?" said Eduardo. "You bet your chess sets I have. Boys, saddle up, Archie just passed the test."

"What's that mean?" I asked.

Eduardo smiled. "It means welcome to the Nimrods, Archie from Omaha. Welcome to the Nimrods."

THE END

Can you help me spread the word about *TALES OF A PIRATE NINJA*? If you enjoyed reading about Archie and his adventures, I would be honored if you asked a parent to help you write a short review about my book where you bought it. Those honest reviews really help readers find my books, and I want to introduce PIRATE NINJA to as many readers as possible. Thank you so much for your help!

~ Daniel Kenney

TURN THE PAGE FOR
EXCITING BONUS MATERIAL!
The First Twenty Pages of
LUNCHMEAT LENNY!

Chapter One

My name is Lenny Parker and I already know what you're thinking. I don't look anything like that tough kid on the cover, do I?

Well, there's an explanation for that. In fact, there's an explanation for practically everything. You see, I never meant to be a crime boss. I just wanted my peanut butter back.

My dad, the Colonel, had moved Mom and me to Wedge City, California, and I was starting my sixth school in six years. The Colonel promised this move would be different, that we might actually stay a few years. And, the Colonel pointed out two more advantages to our new hometown.

First, we'd be only three hours north of San Francisco and the Colonel promised he'd take me to see my beloved San Francisco Giants for the very first time. Second, a brand new amusement park called Danger Mountain was being built just outside of town. Inside of this man-made mountain was going to be a full amusement park complete with a first of its kind mining tunnel rollercoaster. In other words, about the most awesome thing I could imagine.

And so, during the first week of August, the Colonel, my mom, and I moved from Nevada to Northern California. Correction, my mom and I did most of the moving while the Colonel drove ahead so he could take over his new command at Gardner Army Base. And within a few short days, I'd already attended my first day of school.

My new school was McMillan, a huge rectangular red brick building in the center of town with a tall flagpole out front. I suppose it was like the other six schools I'd attended in my life with the exception that it was bigger. And meaner. I was in sixth grade now. I had a locker, walked to all my classes, and saw things I'd never seen before in my life.

On the first day, I walked into the stairwell to see three eighth grade girls giving each other homemade tattoos. One of them growled and told me to move before she kicked me where "the sun don't shine." I didn't want to find out where exactly the "sun don't shine," so I scurried away fast. Another day, I saw a boy with a Mohawk start a trash can on fire in the library, then drop it out of the second-story window where it fell onto the principal's car. And on yet another day, I saw that same boy skateboard down the middle of a cafeteria table filled with girls. By the time he reached the other side of the cafeteria, the school's Head of Discipline, Helmet Kruger, had his hands around the boy, dragging him off to detention.

The boy's name was Eddie, but people called him Spaghetti Eddie. In addition to his weird nickname and strange hairdo, he always wore a long black trench coat, skateboarded to every class, and had what the Colonel would call a bad attitude. I knew because he smarted off in our math class all the time and got detentions on an almost daily basis. In fact, Spaghetti Eddie was everything the Colonel despised and maybe for that reason, I was strangely curious about him.

But I stayed my distance. I always stayed my distance. In the past, I'd made the mistake of making friends only to find out that the Colonel was moving me to yet another town and another school.

I stopped making that mistake three schools ago. Now, I did my time. I stayed out of trouble, tried to get B's, and followed my number one rule.

Never make friends.

I know what you're thinking, how's a kid get along without friends? Not as hard as you think. My mom's nice and she pretty much lets me do what I want. And for a couple of moves I had a pet bullfrog named Cinnamon. That was fun until one night Cinnamon got away from his aquarium, and decided to sleep in the blender. And the next morning when mom went to make her smoothie? Let's just say it was Cinnamon flavored. Not pretty. I've been somewhat traumatized ever since, mom even made me go see a therapist because of the whole thing. I think he diagnosed me with post-traumatic frog disorder.

But thankfully, through it all; through the constant moves, the different schools, the dad who's never there and the exploding bullfrog; there's always been one constant. The one thing I could always count on: beautiful brown color, smooth creamy texture, and deep rich taste.

Peanut butter.

You see, I'm a picky eater. There's not much I eat. But I've always loved peanut butter. Some kids get handed a football or a baseball when they're babies. I think I must have had a spoonful of extra creamy in my crib.

Peanut Butter is the perfect food really. It's a nut and an oil. There's sugar in it, and tons of protein and fat. I do eat other foods. Bread, crackers, basically anything that can act as a peanut butter delivery mechanism. I learned delivery mechanism in some ballistic missile documentary the Colonel made me watch.

One time, we were out of bread at the house, so I cut up pieces of a Nike shoe box and had myself a cardboard peanut butter sandwich. Not as bad as you think. Mom thought I was crazy, but then I showed her the box and the secret message the box had given me. "Mom," I whispered. "The box told me to just do it. So *I did*."

It didn't take me long to fall into a familiar pattern in my unfamiliar town. Every day, I would ride my bike home from school. It gave me a chance to see a little bit of the new town I was in. When I got home every day, I'd fix myself a couple peanut butter sandwiches, do my homework, then watch baseball on the television. And then I would wait. Mom and I would both wait for the Colonel to get home and if he did, he would tell us about how important his job was, and how he knew we understood, and about how hopefully I would grow into the type of man who one day makes him proud.

And sometimes he would look at me and sort of shake his head.

And when I was certain my parents were in bed for the night, I usually would slip down to the kitchen, eat peanut butter straight out of the jar, stare out the window, and wonder whether next year, the next town, and the next school would finally be different.

Chapter Two

On the Monday of my second week at McMillan, I walked from Algebra to Social Studies while focused on a pair of green tennis shoes six feet in front of me. Somebody bumped me from the left. "It's Lenny right?"

I looked over. A girl. She had ridiculous long brown hair that she kept in pig tails, she wore bright blue overalls, had strange looking glasses, and exceptionally big teeth. And she was talking. To me.

"Yes," I said, then put my head back down.

"I'm Megan. But most people call me Mega Bits."

I kept following the green shoes.

"Aren't you going to ask me why?" she asked.

"Not really," I said, keeping my eyes focused on the floor in front of me.

"I'm good with computers." She shrugged. "I guess you could call me a computer genius."

I looked over again and she smiled, her teeth somehow even bigger than I observed the first time. Her upper lip was thin and her lower lip was big. Like they were mismatched.

"Computers have bytes and bits and all that jazz, so that's where it comes from."

"Oh," I managed to finally say.

"So, you're new and I noticed you eating alone during lunch. You should come sit with me and my friends."

I stood in front of Mrs. Hardy's science class and Megan, or whatever she called herself, was bouncing up and down on her tiptoes apparently waiting for me to talk.

"Yeah, well I've got to go," I said, then slipped into class before she could even respond.

I sat alone at lunch and avoided Mega Bits every time she tried to catch my eye. Instead, I focused on my double peanut butter sandwich and the Reese's Peanut Butter Cup I snuck out of my mom's purse. After school, I rode my bike home like usual, but took a detour down Main Street when I noticed a kid with a Mohawk screaming down the middle of the street on his skateboard. Spaghetti Eddie. I followed him down Main Street, and watched as he weaved in and out of cars, hopped onto the curb, jumped his board up onto a planter box, flipped the red and black skateboard into the air, and landed squarely back down on it.

Then Spaghetti Eddie sailed down the sidewalk, his long black trench coat flowing behind him so that you couldn't even see the board and it looked like he was floating sideways down the sidewalk. He was heading for Maple's News Stand and crouched low to the ground as he approached. And as he passed by the front of the newsstand, he reached his hand up, and grabbed a candy bar. Then he kept riding down the street. Mr. Maple never even saw him.

No doubt about it, the Colonel would *definitely* not like Spaghetti Eddie. But me? Had to admit. Still curious.

I kept following him and watched him turn down an alley. I waited a bit, then turned down the alley myself. As soon as I did, something hit me hard and I flew off my bike. I scrambled to get up, but Eddie stepped over me and set his boot onto my chest. He reached in his trench coat, pulled out an enormous alarm clock, wound it up, and set it next to me on the ground.

"You've got thirty seconds to explain."

"Explain what?" I said.

"Why you're following me."

The clock ticked loudly. I squirmed, but Eddie pressed his boot down harder.

"I was curious," I gurgled out.

"About?" he said.

"Who you are and what you do."

"So you're not with the Irish gang?"

"The what?" I said.

"You're not with the Irish?"

"I don't know what you're talking about. My name is Lenny, I'm new in school, and my dad's a Colonel in the army."

Eddie loosened the pressure on my chest. He shook his head.

"I see you follow me again, and I'll hurt you. Got it?"

He grabbed his skateboard, jumped on board, and took off, his trench coat flowing behind him, his dark Mohawk fading in the distance.

I stumbled to my feet, found my bike, and peddled like crazy for home.

Chapter Three

"So, I invite you to my table and you decide to eat by yourself instead?" I looked up. It was Mega Bits. Big teeth.

I shrugged.

"Don't worry, I've decided that since you won't eat with us, I will eat with you today." She sat.

"I'm fine by myself, okay?"

Mega Bits paused, folded her hands and leaned forward.

"Are you? Are you fine by yourself? We get kids like you every year. Your dad's in the military isn't he?"

I paused. "How did you know that?"

"Listen, Lenny, you dress like one of the Hardy boys. You're the only kid in school who has a crease in his khakis and wears short sleeve button-down shirts. I'm guessing your dad is a Colonel, right?"

"You're a good guesser."

"Ha, I didn't guess. I looked you up. You've been to a different school for the last six years. That's a drag."

"You looked me up?" I said, more than a little annoyed.

"So let me ask you—the whole walk around with your head down all the time, is that a defense mechanism or just a sign of low self-esteem?"

"You looked me up?" I said again.

She made a face and pushed against her glasses with her finger. "And I've been watching you. Every day, a peanut butter sandwich and a plastic baggie full of peanut butter that you eat with your finger. A little disgusting and, more to the point, just plain weird."

"Why are you watching me?"

"Lenny, you're not helping yourself out here. You may have been able to get away with this act before, but you're in Junior High now. Junior High is the show. I hear there are bets being placed right now on which guy's going to stuff you into a locker first."

I'd never been stuffed into a locker before. Maybe she was kidding. "Just leave me alone. I'll be fine."

She leaned back in her chair, folded her arms, and got a curious look on her face. "So that's it, isn't it? You try to act invisible. You figure if you don't look at anybody or offend anybody and just keep to yourself—that you'll be fine until the next time your daddy moves."

I stiffened. My face grew warm and my hand clenched around my sandwich. "And *you* can somehow help me?"

She scrunched up her chin. "I can. I'll lead you around, introduce you to people, help you make friends." She jabbed a thumb at her chest. "You stick with me, sixth grade will be a lot more enjoyable."

I looked over at her normal table. Two nerdy girls sat there, giggling over a math book. I shook my head at Mega

Bits.

"Not so sure taking advice from you is such a good idea."

Her face fell, her mouth hanging half open. Then she glared at me and sprung up.

"I thought you might be different, but Lenny, you're no better than the rest of them."

Chapter Four

I avoided Mega Bits the rest of the week, and on Friday raced home after school to get ready. It was the last Giant's game that might work with the Colonel's busy schedule, and he promised to get home early so we could make it to San Francisco on time.

Did I mention the Colonel's not very good at keeping promises? I and my glove waited for him on the front porch and, of course, he never came. Mom eventually came outside to break the news that the Colonel had to work late that night doing maneuvers, whatever those were.

"Sorry bout last night, Lenny," the Colonel said the next morning when I came down to the kitchen. He was polishing his boots. I'm not sure he even looked up when he said it.

I shrugged and walked away. "It's just disappointing," I muttered.

I probably shouldn't have used that word.

"Excuse me," he said in the voice that meant I better stop and look at him immediately. "Disappointing?" he said. He shook his head, snorted, then went back to spit polishing his boots. "Well that's just rich. Lenny, you don't know the meaning of disappointment. Have you ever spent a whole summer in the filthy hot jungle? Ninety-eight days in a row I ate canned tuna on saltine crackers. On day ninety-nine, I ran out of tuna so I spent the day gnawing on my finger. You know what disappointment is? Day one hundred. I was still hungry but in addition to not having food, now I didn't have my finger." He held up his ring finger, the one that was half as long as the others. "You ever experience disappointment like that?"

I was only twelve years old, had never been in the jungle, and had all ten of my fingers. So I guess the Colonel had a point. He also had on his army face. My dad wasn't a yeller. He had perfected this "I'm disappointed in you" face that I called his Army face. What it meant was somebody, usually me, was not up to army standards. His standards.

In fact, I so consistently failed to measure up to Army standards, that I wasn't entirely sure why the Colonel kept me around. He should have adopted a first lieutenant or a shiny green jeep instead. I remember one day in particular, Dad was trying to help me think of things I was good at for a school project. Noticeably stumped, he whacked me on the shoulder. "Well, at least you're the son of a Colonel, so you've got that going for you."

He actually said that to me.

Maybe that's why I started to love peanut butter so much.

And that's also why the Colonel doesn't really need to know about this crime boss thing. Not yet. Maybe when he's real old, and he's using a cane, and wearing an eye patch, and he no longer carries a gun on his waist, and he's hooked up to an oxygen tank, maybe then I'll tell him all about how his son became Lunchmeat Lenny and how I found my extraordinary crew.

The day after the Colonel forgot to take me to the Giants game, he broke more bad news. He had to make an emergency trip overseas. Didn't know for sure when he'd be back, but it would probably be a month at least.

And just like that, Mom and I were alone once more. That night, I snuck down to the kitchen, ate peanut butter from the jar and looked outside. And in the morning, I woke up early, and made my famous peanut butter pancakes. Then before I left for school, I reminded Mom that I just finished up the last of the peanut butter, and handed her a double coupon I'd found in the newspaper.

She smiled and assured me that the pantry would be well stocked by the time I returned from school.

Chapter Five

School was mostly normal that day, except for the commotion in the cafeteria. Some emergency that I didn't know anything about, nor did I care. Normally by the end of a school day, I have serious peanut butter on the brain, I can't think or concentrate on anything else, and I ride my bike home as fast as possible.

That's what I did on this day, but while I weaved in and out of cars, jumped curbs and avoided women with strollers, I noticed something strange. Big green cargo vans were everywhere. And coming out of houses carrying cardboard boxes were guys wearing blue suits and wearing silver sunglasses. It was weird and any other time, I might have cared. But like I said, when PB is on the brain, I'm all in. And I needed to get home.

I noticed a couple more of those green vans on my street, but blew past them, rode into my driveway, and dropped my bike against our front steps. I rushed into the house and ran for the kitchen. Mom was sitting alone at the kitchen table. She looked up and in an instant, I knew. Something was wrong.

She was holding the afternoon paper and had an empty look in her eye. Her lower lip trembled. There was a single tear on her cheek.

Something terrible had happened.

"Lenny?"

"Mom, whatever it is can't be too bad, just let me fix myself a sandwich and then we can talk about it."

All of a sudden, my mom jumped up like a jack-in-the-box and stood in front of me and the pantry. This was weird behavior, especially for my mom.

"Err, Mom, would you mind moving?"

Droplets of sweat collected on her forehead.

"Lenny, you know what I was thinking, why eat peanut butter today? Why not change things up? How about today I take you out for a big hot fudge sundae?"

But Mom wasn't smiling when she said it. She was chewing on the corner of her lip so hard it was starting to bleed. Something was not right.

"You're freaking me out, Mom. After my sandwich we can talk, but I'm starting to get a little dizzy, I need to eat." I reached my hand over her shoulder and grabbed hold of the cabinet door knob.

That's when Mom turned into a crazy person. She grabbed me around the waist in a bear hug and started to lift me away from the pantry. Luckily, I had a good grip and I wasn't about to let go of that door.

She yelled at me to let go, then when that wouldn't work—"don't do it Lenny! Let's go out for ice cream, ice cream is so much better than peanut butter. Or chocolate, how about you just start eating chocolate instead?!"

I kept pulling.

"Or, I could just dump sugar right down your throat, please, Lenny?!"

It's like aliens had abducted my mother, and this lady who was holding onto me was some freakishly strong impostor. At least that's the rationale I used when I did something that I'm not terribly proud of.

I kicked my mom. Hard. Right in the shin. She let go of me immediately, squealed like a stuck pig, and then started hopping around on one foot. Like I said, not proud of it. But at the moment, she was the psycho alien creature keeping a hungry boy away from his peanut butter and I didn't know what else to do.

I opened up the pantry, looked inside, and I felt like I got punched in the gut.

On the left were the boxes of cereal. On the right were the cans of vegetables. But in the middle, the grand middle where the peanut butter was always featured?

Nothing.

No peanut butter. Not one jar. Just a bunch of empty shelf space, mocking me.

Mom had never, and I mean never, forgotten to buy peanut butter before, and that meant something terrible really had occurred. I spun around and mom was just shaking her head, holding onto the newspaper.

"Mom," I said, my voice a little shaky. "Why is there no peanut butter in the pantry?"

She shook her head back and forth, then looked at me with her big brown eyes. "Lenny, I'm just so sorry, I don't know what to say. I went to the grocery store today, and when I did, there were vans outside, a bunch of men in blue suits carrying out boxes and boxes of...." She swallowed hard and started to let out a full-throated sob.

"Peanut butter, Lenny. They were taking it all. I asked the store manager what was going on. He looked at me like I was crazy. 'Haven't you heard what happened?' he said. Then he handed me a newspaper and when I read the headline, I thought I might get sick."

My head was spinning at the possibilities.

"Lenny, I'm sorry. I feel so bad for you."

"What mom, what exactly happened?"

She handed me the newspaper. On the front page in huge block letters was the headline.

I stumbled back in horror, then gathered myself, and read the headline again:

NATIONAL FOOD EMERGENCY
PEANUT BUTTER NO LONGER SAFE

DO YOU WANT TO READ THE REST OF
LUNCHMEAT LENNY 6th GRADE CRIME BOSS?

Available now as an e-book or print book

ALSO WRITTEN BY DANIEL KENNEY

BUY ON AMAZON
www.amzn.com/B00NMSJ16Q

BUY ON AMAZON
www.amzn.com/B00SHYGH6W

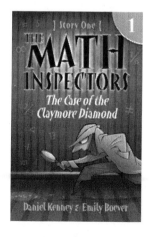

BUY ON AMAZON
www.amzn.com/B00O2AMVW4

BUY ON AMAZON
www.amzn.com/B00SQ20IZQ

BUY ON AMAZON
www.amzn.com/B00SW2TDZ6

ABOUT THE AUTHOR

Daniel Kenney and his wife Teresa live in Omaha, Nebraska with zero cats, zero dogs, one gecko, and lots of kids. When those kids aren't driving him nuts, Daniel is busy writing books, cheering on the Benedictine Ravens, and plotting to take over the world. He is the author of The Beef Jerky Gang, Lunchmeat Lenny, Middle Squad, Dart Guns At Dawn, and the co-author of The Math Inspectors. Found out more information at www.DanielKenney.com.

Made in the USA
San Bernardino, CA
18 March 2016